Captain Tugalong

By **Dee Cache**

Illustrated by **Howard M. Burns**

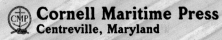 **Cornell Maritime Press**
Centreville, Maryland

Slip number twenty had been empty for a long time, just like the cabin of Captain Tugalong, the tugboat in slip twenty-one. Once, Tugalong had been the pride of the harbor. His *lines* held him safely tied to the dock. His captain always checked for worn spots on the lines. If he found any, he replaced that line right away. "Those were the good old days," the tugboat said softly as tears fell over his *bow*.

When Captain Tugalong was new, he traveled up and down the harbor directing big ships in and out safely. One time, a boat was coming straight toward him. His captain blew the whistle once, steered to *starboard,* and passed with the other boat on his *port* side. There wasn't a crash because both boats knew a whistle signal of one short blast meant the two boats would pass port-side to port-side.

Now tied in his slip, Tugalong could feel his cabin jiggle with broken glass and cracked wood. He could feel the wiring toss to and fro on windy nights. Sad and lonely he sat, year after year, with his *stern* low in the water. Then something happened to change his life.

A *wake* made the tugboat toss and roll. "What's going on here?" he yelled. A boat had passed the dock too fast, and waves pounded the sides of the poor old tugboat. Water splashed into *portholes* that had been broken for years. Then Captain Tugalong saw a boat headed toward the dock.

"Careful! Take it slow," someone was yelling. "Toss the *fenders* out now," the voice said.

slip—the space between two piers where a boat is tied
line—rope, when used on a boat
bow—the front or forward part of the boat
starboard—the right side of the boat, when looking forward
port—the left side of the boat, when looking forward
stern—the rear part of the boat
wake—waves made by a moving boat
porthole—a window on a boat
fender—a cushion to protect the boat

Tugalong saw the most beautiful sight he had seen in many years. A lovely sleek sailboat was coming toward him, sparkling in the noonday sun.

"Oh no! She's going to hit me!" the tugboat cried. "If I still had my horn, I could blast it five times very quickly to warn her she may be in danger," he thought.

Luckily, the sailboat slowed down, as a voice shouted, "Slip twenty is ours. Let's take her in carefully." Soon, Tugalong's new neighbor was sitting right next to him.

A young boy wearing a *life jacket* looked through binoculars to get a clearer view of the harbor. Captain Tugalong was glad to see the boy wore deck shoes because it might be dangerous for him to be barefoot on a boat. He could stub his toe or slip on the wet surface.

A woman stepped carefully from the boat to the dock. She quickly tied up the boat. She wore a bright yellow jacket with "Sun Dancer" printed on it.

The old tugboat stared at the beautiful sailboat. He remembered how people admired him when he was new. "She probably won't even talk to me," Tugalong thought. He wished he didn't have to meet her. He felt so ugly.

"Good morning, neighbor," a musical voice called out the next morning. "Who are you?"

The tugboat was so shocked he could hardly speak. She was talking to him, and it would be rude not to answer her. "Cap . . . Captain . . . Captain Tugalong," he whispered.

life jacket or life vest—a special jacket or vest that helps a person float, also called a personal flotation device (PFD)

"What?" she said.

"My name is Captain Tugalong, and I am a tugboat," he said a wee bit louder.

"Hi, Captain. How long have you been here?" she asked.

"Years and years and years," he replied.

"My name is Sun Dancer. I wondered who my new neighbor would be, and I am so happy it's you. You look so wise, maybe you will share some of your adventures with me so I can learn more about the sea." Sun Dancer smiled and blinked her long eyelashes at Tugalong as she spoke.

The tugboat was very surprised. He had a new neighbor who was a lovely sailboat, and she wanted to be his friend. He knew that he had found someone to talk with and enjoy. Captain Tugalong slept peacefully that night, with no more tears. As the neighborhood fish swam under the old boat, they thought they heard the old tug snoring lightly.

As weeks passed, Tugalong and Sun Dancer traded stories about their builders, their captains, and their adventures. The tug listened carefully while Sun Dancer told him she was built in America, and she was very proud of her sleek lines. He listened even when he was very tired.

"What emergency equipment do you have on board, Captain?" asked the sailboat.

"None anymore," Tugalong answered. "I used to be well stocked, but over the years, people came aboard and took all my equipment. What do you have on board, Sun Dancer?"

"I have PFDs in many sizes and shapes. Some look like vests, and some look like jackets. If anyone falls in the water, a PFD helps the person to float and to stay warm until help arrives. Everyone on board has a PFD with his or her name on it. There's a PFD that looks like a giant donut! It's called a life ring or throwable device.

"The first aid kit is kept in a place where everyone can find it easily. It contains bandages, gauze, tape, and lots of items needed when someone is hurt. A flashlight and extra batteries are handy too, ready to use at night.

"A compass shows which direction the boat is going. One is mounted at the steering place; another is held by hand.

"*Flares* are stowed away safely. I also have three fire extinguishers in good working order. They can be reached quickly and easily to put out a fire.

"Did I tell you that my captain teaches his family how to use all the equipment safely?" Sun Dancer asked.

Captain Tugalong was glad to hear that, and told Sun Dancer, "The captain is always in charge, no matter what. Everyone must listen to the captain and follow his orders."

Sun Dancer, or Sunnie, as Captain Tugalong called her, returned one night from a long trip at sea. The tug was glad to see her. He missed her when she was not by his side.

"I'm very happy to see you, Sun Dancer. You are very special," he told the sleepy sailboat.

"Hi there, my friend; I'm glad to be home," said Sunnie.

flare—a bright flame used to signal for help

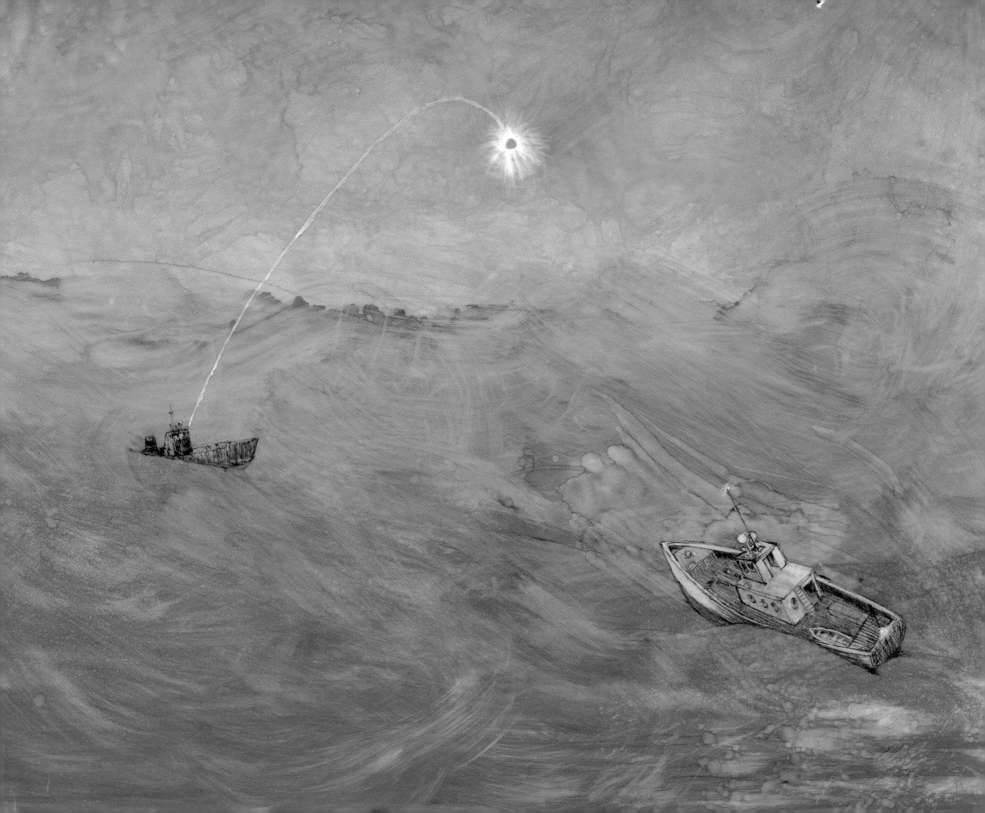

"It was too quiet while you were gone," Tugalong said laughingly.

Later, Sunnie quizzed the tug. "What do you think is the most important thing to know about boating?"

Captain thought carefully before answering. "Uh . . . ahh . . . there are so many things. I'll think about which is the most important and let you know."

Soon, Tugalong had an answer. "Sunnie, I believe the most important things to know about safe boating are the rules of the road. There are many, but here's a list of the basic rules that everyone should know before going out on a boat."

1. When two powerboats traveling in opposite directions meet, both should steer to starboard so they will pass port-side to port-side.
2. When two powerboats approach at an angle, the boat that is to starboard of the other is the *stand-on* boat, and the boat that is to port is the *give-way* boat.
3. When two boats approaching each other are a sailboat and a powerboat, usually the sailboat is the stand-on boat, and the powerboat is the give-way boat.
4. If a sailboat is using its motor, it follows the same rules as a powerboat.
5. When two sailboats approach each other and one is on *starboard tack* and the other is on *port tack,* the boat on starboard tack is the stand-on boat.

stand-on boat—the boat that should hold its course
give-way boat—the boat that should change its course

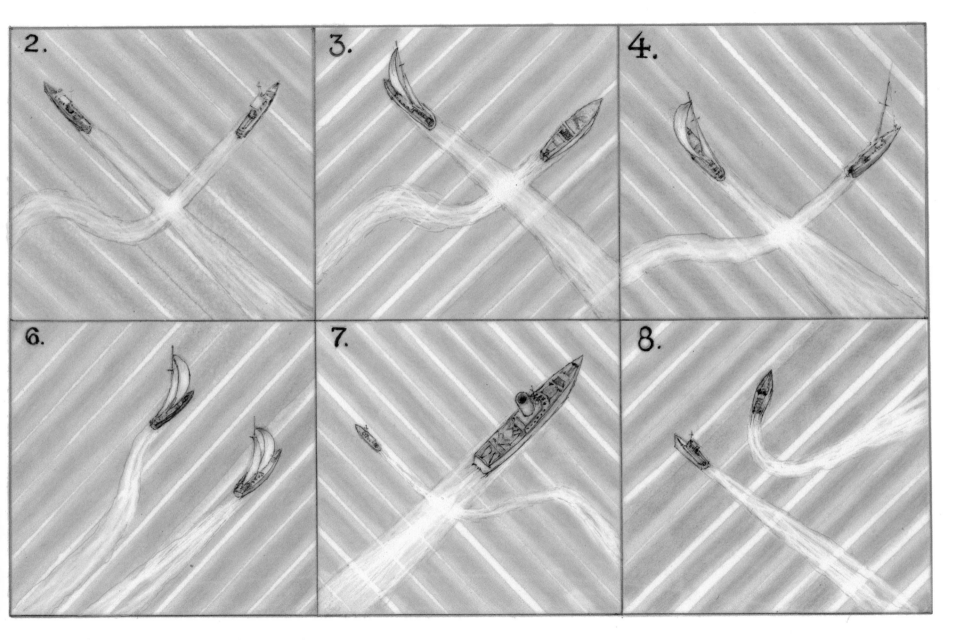

starboard tack—sailing with the wind
   coming from the right side of the
   boat
port tack—sailing with the wind coming
   from the left side of the boat

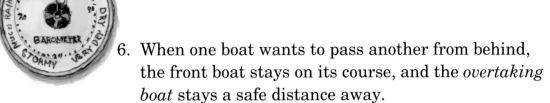

6. When one boat wants to pass another from behind, the front boat stays on its course, and the *overtaking boat* stays a safe distance away.

7. All pleasure boats should stay out of the way of freighters, tugboats, commercial fishing boats, or other large boats because these boats cannot change direction quickly and cannot stop in a short distance.

8. Remember that another boater may not know the rules. Even if your boat should be the stand-on boat, always be alert, and change course if necessary to avoid hitting another boat.

One stormy night, Tugalong heard Sun Dancer saying, "Wake up, please. I want to talk to you."

"What a night," the tugboat said. "At least the rain and wind will wash off some of my dirt!" he joked.

"Be serious, Captain," said Sunnie. "I want to ask for help. I'm so confused about the terms boaters use. I want to know them all, but I'm afraid I'll never learn. Will you please help me learn the terms?" And so her lessons began.

"The bow is the front of the boat, the stern is the rear. *Fore* means toward the front of the boat, and *aft* means toward the rear of the boat. As you face forward, starboard is to the right, and port is to the left." Tugalong noticed that Sunnie was listening to every word he said. He continued, "*Windward* is the direction the wind is blowing from, and *leeward* is the direction opposite or away from the wind."

overtaking boat—the boat that is passing another boat
fore—at the front or forward part of a boat
aft—at the rear part of the boat
windward—the direction the wind blows from
leeward—the direction away from the wind

"Wow! How am I ever going to learn all those words?" Sunnie asked. Captain Tugalong was very smart. He knew that it takes time to learn the terms. He suggested they sing the words over and over until Sunnie knew them by heart. Tugalong glowed with pride at his wonderful idea. He and Sunnie sang for many hours until a dreary fog rolled in and covered everything.

In the distance, the sound of a fog horn came from the lighthouse at the harbor entrance. Boaters know how close they are to a lighthouse because they hear the fog horn sounding louder and louder as they get closer and closer.

Fog horns, bells, and whistles use their own special language to help boaters avoid danger. For example, when a big boat backs out of a slip, it sounds three short blasts to let others know the boat is going *astern.* And, just as a one-blast signal means a boat is steering to starboard, a two-blast signal means the boat is going to port.

"Once a new crewmember was on board when there was an emergency at sea," the tugboat said. "Are you too tired to listen?" he asked Sunnie.

"You know I want to hear all your stories," she said.

"Well, it was long ago, but the same rules still apply. We were at sea when something scraped my *hull.* Water was leaking inside. We needed help. The new crewmember was steering at the time. He was worried about the leak and was not sure what to do first. Then the captain came into

astern—boat is moving backward, in reverse
hull—body of a boat

the *wheelhouse* and said, "Listen to me, everyone." His voice was so powerful that everyone on board knew he was serious.

"The captain told a crewman to put up the *distress flag* as a signal for help. Then he went to the radiotelephone and turned the dial to channel 16, the marine radio's calling channel. He spoke very slowly and very clearly, saying, '*Mayday . . . Mayday . . . Mayday.*'

"Sunnie, are you listening?" Tugalong whispered. But it was no use; the beautiful sailboat was fast asleep.

The next morning, Sunnie asked Tugalong about the night before. "What were you saying about channel 16?"

"I was telling you a story, but you fell asleep before I finished. Did you hear anything?" the tug asked.

"I didn't hear the ending. Please tell me again. I'll listen this time," Sunnie promised.

"O.K." the tug said. "The captain told a crewman to put up the distress flag to show other boats that we needed help. Then he went to the radiotelephone and turned the dial to channel 16. He spoke very slowly and very clearly, saying, 'Mayday . . . Mayday . . . Mayday.' You know, Sunnie, even though there are many different kinds of radiotelephones, all of them have one channel to use when there's an emergency, and that's channel 16."

"I know, I know. Now please get on with the story," Sun Dancer said impatiently.

wheelhouse—on some boats, the place where a person steers
distress flag—a flag with a black square and a black circle on an orange background
Mayday—radio distress call; it means "help me"

"The captain turned to channel 16 on the radiotelephone and said 'Mayday . . . Mayday . . . Mayday. This is Captain Murray on the tugboat Captain Tugalong.' Then he gave our position, described nearby landmarks, and explained what was wrong. He reported how many people were on board and said no one was hurt. He repeated the message over and over, but no one answered for a while. Finally a voice on channel 16 said help was on the way."

"Whew! What a close call. You were lucky the radio call brought help so quickly," Sunnie said.

Sun Dancer told Tugalong that her captain explains to his family how important it is to understand all the equipment on board. "Sometimes the captain and crew pretend something is wrong; then everyone practices what to do in case of a real emergency.

"Did you have captains like mine?" she asked.

Tugalong recalled several and spent the entire day telling stories about captains he had known over the years.

The tugboat had been thinking and dreaming a lot lately. He sat silently in the water as weeks passed.

"I wish I could be seaworthy like you," he told his friend. "Wouldn't it be wonderful if I could work again?"

"Oh, one day you'll sparkle and look better than ever. If you believe something wonderful is going to happen, it will. If you want something—really want it—you'll see, it will happen. I just know it," Sunnie told the sad tugboat.

Months passed. Sun Dancer sailed away for weeks at a time. When she returned from each trip, she found the tugboat looking worse and worse. "The ocean is finding new ways to sneak inside me," Tugalong complained. "I have so many holes that every day more and more water comes in. When I was a very busy working tugboat and had a few small leaks, the captain would stuff towels or rags into the holes until I could be repaired. In an emergency, stuffing a larger hole with pillows or blankets is O.K., but it isn't the proper way to repair a boat."

"I know that," Sunnie said as she listened to her friend creak and watched him slip deeper and deeper into the water each day. "Who owns you now?" she asked.

"My last owner was Captain Sydney. He was very old. He went away and never came back again. Then a stranger came aboard and put a 'For Sale' sign on me. I've been sitting here ever since," Tugalong told her.

Seasons passed. Sun Dancer sailed away often. When she returned from one trip, she was very excited.

"Captain . . . Captain Tugalong. . . you should have seen what happened to me on our last trip," the sailboat squealed as she was being tied up in her slip. "There was no wind, and the captain needed to turn on the engine so we could get home. We were low on fuel, and the family was really worried."

"What happened? Are you all right?" the tug asked.

"First the captain checked my battery, and then he worked on the engine. The family was glad he knew how to repair things. They said they felt safe sailing with him at the *helm.* I feel secure with my captain too. Tomorrow, people from a *boatyard* are taking me out of the water. If I need any repairs, they'll fix me so I am like new again."

Tugalong was very upset. Sunnie bragged about her captain, but he didn't even know his owner. The tugboat wept and hoped he'd sink into the sea forever.

The next day, some people stood on the dock staring at Tugalong. "Hey, J.B.!" one man shouted. "Look at all the cracks in the wood. This tug will take a lifetime to fix up."

J.B. examined every detail of the old boat. He knew this was a special boat. He opened his wallet and glanced at a picture of his Grandpa Bill standing by a boat very much like Tugalong. The twinkle in his grandfather's eyes was reason enough for J.B. to consider buying this old boat.

"You think this isn't a good idea, but there's something special about this old tug," J.B. told his friend Mike.

J.B.'s friends couldn't understand why anyone would want to buy a broken-down tug, especially this one. Lori, Diane, and Eve lagged behind the rest of the group. They whispered so J.B. wouldn't hear what they were saying. "I'll bet this old boat was really a beauty when it was new, but look at it now! What a mess! You don't think J.B. will buy it, do you?" They all shook their heads in disbelief.

helm—wheel or tiller, used to steer a boat
boatyard—a place where boats are repaired

"What a beauty," J.B. told his wife Maria. "When I was a little boy, my grandpa used to take me aboard his tugboat. He called it Honey B. He loved that boat and spent more time on Honey B than any place else." And with that, J.B., Maria, and Mike walked down the dock and climbed aboard Captain Tugalong.

"I must be dreaming; it just can't be," the tug told the neighborhood fish. "Somebody's here to look at me."

What a perfect day it was. The sky was clear blue with just a few puffy white clouds overhead. Weekend sailors were hustling about, preparing their boats for short trips up and down the shore. And Tugalong would soon have a new owner.

The next day, J.B. came back to the harbor with a man named Dan, who was a marine surveyor. Dan was an expert on boats. He inspected every inch of the tugboat. He shined his flashlight into the tiniest cracks and holes. He poked and pulled on everything and made lots of notes on his clipboard. Then he told J.B. what repairs were needed to make Tugalong look new again.

Tugalong was so glad to have people aboard, he didn't even mind all the poking. Finally, the tugboat had a new captain, one who would love him and who planned to spend his whole life with him. Sun Dancer was so happy. "Oh my dear, dear friend, I told you not to give up. I just knew you'd be a handsome tugboat one day."

"Oh sure," the tugboat fibbed. "I knew it all the time," and he winked at her.

J.B. liked to spend time aboard his new tugboat, singing, whistling, sometimes just sitting on the bow and smiling from ear to ear. He replaced all the broken glass in the portholes. The new glass looked like diamonds. He made a list of all the repairs he wanted to do and nailed the list right over a porthole. Then he began the long job of making Tugalong as good as new.

Weekends, nights, or holidays, J.B. was always working on Tugalong. Sometimes his friends Mike and Tom would help with the work, but mostly J.B. worked alone or with Maria. He lovingly patched holes and repaired parts, tearing off the old and replacing with the new. He was delighted with the way the boat was shaping up. The neighborhood fish were happy too. They swam around Tugalong and Sun Dancer, sometimes leaping out of the water in an excited dance of happiness.

J.B.'s Grandpa Bill had collected a lot of sea-captain's hats, old ship's bells, and whistles for over fifty years, and he'd given the collection to J.B. The brass bells and whistles were tarnished and covered with dirt and grime. The hats were all clean because each one had been carefully wrapped. J.B. decided to bring them all aboard the tug. He also brought a few paintings of old ships; he wanted to hang one of these in the wheelhouse.

J.B. and Mike polished all the bells until they could see themselves in the shiny surface. They put a lot of hooks on the walls and installed a little light over each hook. When they had hung all the old bells, whistles, and hats, they stood back and admired all the beautiful things.

One day after lunch, Mike brought a large telescope to slip number twenty-one and put it on board the tug. J.B., Maria, and Mike mounted it securely to the deck.

"I have the greatest idea," Maria said with excitement in her voice. "Why don't we tell everyone about the interesting things you have on board the tugboat? I know people will come from all over just to see them."

J.B. loved the idea. "We'll make Captain Tugalong into a floating museum, and we can operate it together. What a terrific idea. Why don't we get started today!"

Hearing that, Sun Dancer gave the tug her biggest smile. Captain Tugalong replied with a wink, sending her a silent message that he was glad to be her friend. Tugalong and Sun Dancer had been through good times and bad times, and they were the best of friends. "It's so good to know you are happy again," Sunnie said as she sailed by.

Tugalong was glowing with pride. He was a brand-new boat again. He had a captain who cared about him, and who would take care of him. Soon he would be a floating museum and would continue to show others about boating. Captain Tugalong knew he would never be lonely again.